BATTLE BUGS

THE CHAMELEON ATTACK

by **JACK PATTON**

illustrated by **BRETT BEAN**

SCHOLASTIC INC.

With special thanks to Adrian Bott

Text copyright © 2015 by Hothouse Fiction
Cover and interior art by Brett Bean, copyright © 2015 by Scholastic Inc.

All rights reserved. Published by Scholastic Inc., *Publishers since 1920*, 557 Broadway, New York, NY 10012, by arrangement with Hothouse Fiction. Series created by Hothouse Fiction.

No part of this work may be reproduced, stored in a retrieval system, or transmitted in any form or by any means, electronic, mechanical, photocopying, recording, or otherwise, without written permission of the publisher. For information regarding permission, write to Hothouse Fiction, The Old Truman Brewery, 91 Brick Lane, London E1 6QL, UK.

ISBN 978-0-545-70784-8

10 9 8 7 6   18 19

Printed in the U.S.A.   40
First printing 2015
Book design by Phil Falco and Ellen Duda

CONTENTS

BIRTHDAY BUG

Max Darwin shuffled down the driveway toward his mom's car, keeping his black cape wrapped tightly around him.

His mom looked at her watch, rolled her eyes, and opened the passenger door. "Hurry up, or we'll be late for the birthday party!"

"I'm coming!" Max protested, bunny-hopping the rest of the way and wriggling into the backseat. He could have moved a lot faster if he'd just let the cape go loose, but that would have ruined everything. Carefully, he set his backpack down beside him, not revealing the slightest glimpse of what might be inside his costume.

"I know you want to surprise Tyler, but I don't know why you can't let *me* see what you're wearing." His mom sighed, starting up the car and accelerating onto the road. "After all, you did raid my fabric stash to make it!"

"I'm pupating," Max insisted, as if that explained everything.

"Oh, right," his mom continued. "So you can't come out of your cocoon too soon?"

"Exactly!" Max grinned, jiggling with excitement as his mom drove them through the streets toward Tyler's house. He already knew what his best friend would be dressed as. Tyler was just as obsessed with super-heroes as Max was with bugs. But Max's costume had been a closely guarded secret so far.

"How about I guess?" his mom suggested.

Max just groaned—she'd never be able to figure it out.

"Let's see. A pretty butterfly?"

"Nope," Max said.

"Hmm. Maybe . . . a moth?"

"Wrong again."

"Something nastier? A wasp?"

Max laughed. "No. You'll just have to wait!"

"Fine, fine, you win. I give up." His mom laughed. "Now, where are we? Furze Avenue . . . oh. Oh, no!"

Max sat bolt upright. "What's wrong, Mom?"

"Tyler's present!" she wailed. "I don't remember putting it in the car. Last time I saw it, it was on the kitchen table! We need to turn the car around . . ."

"Wait!" Max called, already rummaging inside his backpack. He pulled out the long, gift-wrapped package—a light-up power sword he'd chosen for Tyler.

"Got it!" he shouted. "It's right here."

"Phew," his mom said. "Crisis averted. It's a good thing one of us has their head screwed on right!"

While he had his backpack open, Max felt inside for the huge, heavy shape of his *Encyclopedia of Arthropods*. Sure enough, the book was in there, along with the magnifying glass that went with it. Ever since his mom had brought it back from an estate auction, the book had never been far from Max's side.

The mysterious old book was not only full of bugs of all different types that Max could look up, it was also full of a strange magic, capable of transporting Max to an amazing world of talking bugs. He'd already had adventures on Bug Island, and the bugs could need him back at a moment's notice.

His mom glanced back at him and groaned. "Do you have to bring that dusty old encyclopedia everywhere you go?"

"Of course," Max said. "Bugs are everywhere!"

"Sometimes I worry you might turn into a bug overnight," his mom joked.

Max couldn't think of anything cooler!

As they pulled up outside Tyler's house, they could hear music blasting from the backyard. Still hugging his black cape close to his body, Max jumped out of the car and sprinted down the path that ran alongside the house. He almost collided with Tyler, who was running the other way.

"Max! You're here!"

"Happy birthday!" Max called, looking Tyler up and down. "Awesome costume!" Tyler looked like he belonged on the cover of a comic book, with his scarlet cape, blue bodysuit, and mask.

"Thanks," Tyler said. "But this isn't all . . . You have to check out my Fortress of Power."

"Your *what*?"

Tyler practically dragged Max into the backyard, where a huge crowd of their school friends had already gathered. Everyone was in costume: from pirates to zombies to ice princesses.

Rising above them all was Tyler's jungle gym. It was a set of two wooden towers with a slide, rope ladders, and a walkway between the two. For Tyler's birthday, it had been transformed into a fortress. Plastic sheets with brick patterns changed the wooden walls into castle ramparts. There were even realistic flame-effect electric torches flickering from the tower tops.

"We're going to have the best siege ever," Tyler said. "Dad's been making ammo all day."

"Ammo?"

"Water balloons. It'll be *total chaos*."

"Count me in!" Max said, glancing around to see his mom and Tyler's mom hurrying over.

"Do I get to see your costume before I go?" Max's mom asked.

"Come on Max, what's under the cape?" Tyler urged.

Max took a deep breath, counted to three, and unfurled his cape with a flourish. The inside was painted a bright orange, with two black dots on either side and a line across the middle—just like a pair of eyes and a mouth. Little extra legs made from stuffed black socks dangled along his sides. The whole thing looked like a giant human face, sure to scare away any bug predators.

"I'm a man-faced stinkbug," he said, beaming proudly. "Cool, huh?"

Tyler stared, too amazed to laugh.

Max's mom just chuckled. "I never would have guessed that! But I think it's more like a *boy*-faced stinkbug."

Everyone burst out laughing.

Max's mom turned his way. "Okay, stink-bug. I'll pick you up at six."

"See ya, Mom," Max said as he headed to the Fortress of Power with Tyler.

"Hold on a sec," Tyler's mom called. "You might want to put your things inside, first."

"Okay," Max agreed. "I'm just dropping off my bag," he called to Tyler.

Max hurried across the deck and into the house. All the bags had been piled up in the corner of the kitchen, and the table was laden with presents for Tyler. Max pulled his backpack open, fished out his own present from under the glowing ency-clopedia, and put it on top of the pile.

Wait. *Glowing* encyclopedia?

He quickly double-checked. No mistake—the pages were pulsing with an eerie greenish light. That meant the Battle Bugs were calling him!

Great timing, Max thought. *The party will just have to wait!*

He couldn't risk being discovered. Even though everyone was outside in the yard, someone might wander in and see Max vanishing into the pages of his book.

With the encyclopedia under his arm, Max went through the house checking all the doors. Luckily, he spotted a closet under the stairs. He pushed through the door and found himself in a small space where old coats and boxes of clutter had been stored.

There were even some nice, thick spider-webs at the back. *Perfect!*

Max shut the door carefully, making as little noise as he could. He took off his cape with the attached legs. It would really slow him down on Bug Island! Then he sat cross-legged among the boxes, opened the encyclopedia to the map of Bug Island, and took out his magnifying glass.

Everything began to swirl around him, faster and faster, like bathwater going down the drain. He felt himself shrinking smaller and smaller as the map loomed up before him, and he vanished inside.

CLOSE CALL

Max shut his eyes tight and braced himself for the impact. Every time he fell onto Bug Island, he always landed with a bump.

But this time, he didn't. The feeling of falling just kept going on and on. Wind whistled past his face.

Puzzled, he opened his eyes and looked around . . .

"Aaaaaaaargh!"

The yell of panic burst out of him before he could stop it. He was falling out of the sky! He was plummeting like a skydiver who'd just jumped out of a plane—and he didn't even have a parachute!

Max looked down as the green jungle and the glittering sea of Bug Island came rushing up toward him. By sheer luck he was above the bay, where it looked like the sea had taken a big blue bite out of the land. If he could land in the water, he might have a chance.

He spread his arms and legs out, trying to control his fall. The cove loomed bigger and bigger beneath him.

I'm going to splat like a bug on a

windshield, Max thought. *I have to do something!*

Then he realized, if he curled himself up into a ball, maybe he could shoot through the waves like a speeding bullet.

I hope this works, he thought as he tucked his arms and legs up tight.

As the water loomed up in front of him, Max took a deep breath and braced himself for impact. The next moment, he slammed into the surface.

THOOOOM! Max plunged under the waves with a roaring rush of noise. He tumbled through a shadowy, watery world with bubbles streaming around him, salt water flooding his nose and mouth.

Kicking his legs and thrashing his arms, Max powered to the surface and took a big gulp of air.

"Blurgh-gh!" he gasped, spitting out a mouthful of salty water. He rubbed the sea-foam out of his eyes and looked around. Max couldn't believe his luck—he'd survived!

He took a look around as the waves bobbed him up and down. Luckily, he was close to the shoreline, with the lava bridge a ways off to the left of him and huge cliffs to his right. Even in his soaking wet clothes, he could swim to dry land easily. He began a front crawl through the gentle waves.

As Max swam toward the shore, he spotted a group of bugs on the sand, looking out to sea. They must have been the ones who'd called him here. As he peered into the distance, he was sure he could make out the familiar shape of General Barton, the titan beetle, looming over the other troops.

"Guys!" he yelled happily as he swam. "I'm coming as fast as I can!"

Then he noticed something strange. The bugs looked like they were doing a sort of dance, waving their legs and pincers and antennae and hopping around.

What are they up to? Max thought. *Some kind of bug beach party?* Max liked the idea of playing volleyball against a team of crickets.

However, the closer he swam, the more frantic the bugs became. They were yelling at him now. He could just make out General Barton's deep voice booming across the water, and suddenly his blood turned cold.

"Max, look out!"

"What?" he called.

"Lizard!"

Lizard! The bugs were trying to warn him!

Max turned his head and looked behind him. He gasped in horror. There, on one of the rocks surrounding the bay, sat the unmistakable shape of a lizard basking in the sun.

Max felt a surge of fear as he recognized what the lizard was and understood why the bugs were panicking. From the curved frill on its head and its bright green color, the reptile could be only one thing: a basilisk lizard. And basilisk lizards, he knew, had a very special trick up their scaly sleeves: They could run on water!

"Uh-oh," Max muttered.

As if on cue, the lizard slithered down from the rock. It launched itself across the water, skimming briskly across the waves on its back legs. It was heading right for him!

"Get out of there!" roared General Barton.

"I'm coming!" Max cried, putting on a burst of speed.

Max knew he'd be snapped up in seconds if the lizard caught him. He swam with all the strength he had, straining to reach the shoreline that was still far away. The basilisk moved across the water with unbelievable speed, racing over the surface like an Olympic runner, claws outstretched.

Coughing and spluttering, Max struggled on. He pummeled the water with his best front crawl, but he wasn't going to make it to the shore, and the basilisk lizard must have known it. It bore down on him, hissing, only seconds away now.

The shadow of the lizard fell over him. "I've got you now!" it hissed, lunging out with its claws.

Max braced himself for the lizard's jaws to close around him.

Then, out of nowhere, a gigantic spider came skittering out across the water. Max barely had time to wonder how it was able to run on the surface before the spider crashed into the basilisk. Startled, the lizard lost its rhythm and plunged under the water, struggling and gasping.

"Go!" the spider urged him in a strange, bubbling voice. "Leave the reptile to me!"

Max didn't need telling twice. He swam hard for shore, gasping with the effort, until at last he struggled into the shallows. General Barton, the leader of the Battle Bug army, gently gripped him with his huge pincers,

picked him up, and carried him safely up the beach.

Breathing heavily and soaking wet, Max rested flat on his back for a moment. Then, once he'd gotten his breath back, he sat up and wrung the water out of his costume.

"Thanks, Barton. I thought I was finished back there."

"Don't mention it," Barton said modestly, giving his huge beetle wings an airing.

"What *was* that on the water?" Max asked.

"Ah!" Barton looked pleased with himself. "You've just been introduced to my newest recruits: the fishing spiders. Impressive, don't you think?"

"Very!" Max laughed. Down at the shore, the fishing spider who'd saved his life was scuttling up the beach toward them, shaking the water off its long brown legs.

"Instead of balancing on a web, they balance on water," Barton explained. "They can detect tiny vibrations in the water and rush across to attack prey. That makes them the perfect arachnids to patrol the shore."

Max nodded. The basilisk lizard was only able to run on the water as long as it kept moving, but the spider could stay balanced indefinitely by spreading its weight.

"We need all the help we can get patrolling the shores," Barton continued. "There's even recruits dug into the sand below your feet, ready to attack."

"Cool!" Max cried. "Can I see them?"

"All in good time. They're my secret weapon." Barton chuckled. He gently poked at the bug design on Max's shirt. "I see you're finally becoming one of us!"

"Sorry, it's only a shirt."

"Ah. What a pity. Maybe if you grew some wings, we wouldn't need to keep saving you all the time."

Max laughed.

Barton bowed his head, turning serious. "We need your help, though, Max. The lizards are more of a problem than ever."

"I thought you might. What's the trouble this time?"

General Barton paced back and forth. "We need to improve defenses here on Bug

Island. The lizards are still coming across the lava bridge, and they're setting up bases here before we can react. They're even crossing the water, as you've seen."

"What about the fireflies? Can't they send warnings out?" Max knew all about the secret underground intelligence network that passed information around the island.

"Not if we don't see the lizards coming." Barton sighed. "And that's the trouble. They always catch us unawares. We need some way of spotting them before they attack."

Max looked around the Bug Island bay, trying to think what the bugs could do. Cliffs rose up on either side of the water, almost rivaling the distant Fang Mountain in height. For some reason, he thought of Tyler's birthday party and the Fortress of Power.

Right then, an idea struck him.

"Of course!" he yelled. "It's obvious!"

CLIFF CLIMB

"Well, spit it out, then," Barton cried. "What should we do?"

"Look around us," Max said. "We're surrounded by giant cliffs."

The bugs were camped out on the edge of the beach, the waves lapping toward them. They'd built little more than a few mounds of earth with praying mantises perched on them, looking out to sea—they could definitely use more defenses.

"What if we built a fortress watchtower on the top of Howling Cliffs?" Max suggested. "That way we'd have a clear view of the lava bridge *and* the water, and we could spot the lizards if any more of them tried to cross over."

Max thought back to the fateful day when the volcano had erupted. For years, the sea had separated Bug Island and Reptile Island from one another, and the bugs had lived in peace. But lava flowing down from the volcano had cooled into a rock bridge between the islands, and Bug Island's problems had begun.

General Komodo, the reptile commander, was as sneaky as he was brutal. His lizard forces were constantly crossing the lava bridge and making trouble for the bugs. Some of the lizards, like the chameleons, were camouflage experts—it was tricky to spot them.

"If we got the termite builders on the case, they'd have it done in no time," Max continued.

"Good thinking," Barton said. "I like the sound of that!"

Together, they made their way across the sand toward the beach fortifications. The mantis sentries at the camp saluted and let them through. Inside, Max spotted his old bug friends: Spike, Webster, and Buzz.

"Morning, Max!" shouted Spike, the emperor scorpion. "You're soaking wet! Been for a nice swim?"

"Don't be s-s-silly," stammered Webster, the shy trap-door spider. "Didn't you hear? It was dreadful! Max nearly got . . . he nearly got . . ."

"Nearly got eaten," droned Buzz, the giant hornet. "I'm sorry, Max. I only just heard. My squadron was on nectar break after a long patrol."

"Don't worry about it." Max patted Buzz's bristly thorax.

"The one time he falls out of the sky, and I wasn't there to save him!" Buzz grumbled to herself.

"Don't worry," Barton said firmly. "Now we have a plan—those lizards won't catch us unawares again. Webster! Send the rest of the fishing spiders out on patrol. Now that we've seen one basilisk lizard, there could be more."

"R-right away, sir!" whispered Webster, springing to action.

With the fishing spiders on duty, Barton quickly explained Max's plan to the others.

"We should start work on it right away," Max said.

Barton nodded. "Agreed. You and Spike work well together, so I'm pairing you up to take charge of the construction. I'll send Buzz to check on your progress later in the day."

"Yes, sir!" Spike raised a pincer in salute.

Barton assigned a group of fierce-looking soldier termites to act as bodyguards, then called for the termite builders. "Max will be giving you your orders," he told the foreman. "Obey him just as you would me—we must be quick; there could be another lizard attack at any time."

Razorjaw, the lead soldier termite, called out to his fellow termites: "Okay, everyone! We've got a job to do, so let's get to it!"

"Hop on, shorty," Spike told Max. "Let's get this fortress built."

As the sun rose high above the Howling Cliffs, Max and Spike led the way across the baking-hot beach. Two different types of termite followed: One, the soldier termites, had strong-looking pincers that made them excellent guards for the journey. The other, the workers, had pointy mouthparts and looked much less fearsome. However, they were formidable builders, and were sure to construct the fortress watchtower fast.

Since all the bugs could climb, Max figured it made the most sense to go to the foot of the cliffs and then climb straight up, instead of taking the riskier long way around.

"But you're not a bug," Spike said. "Are you going to be okay?'

"I'll make it," Max said, feeling confident.

The foliage at the bottom of the cliffs was thick, tangled, and hard to get through. It was hot, difficult work, and Max soon dried off under the intense sun. The big climb was still to come. He began to wonder if he should have taken the long way around after all.

Then Spike's next words made him feel even worse. "You be careful on those rocks, human bean," the scorpion said. "Bugs have seen all sorts of lizards on the cliffs lately, and you're always getting yourself into scrapes with them!"

"I'll be careful," Max promised. "That basilisk lizard I met . . . do you think there are more coming?"

"Maybe," Spike said. "Probably. They don't have to come *all* the way over the lava bridge. They can get near the end, then run off across the water and hide up the beach where we can't see them."

"Of course." Max groaned.

"This watchtower idea is fantastic," Spike said cheerfully. "We'll be able to see them coming from a mile away! And Barton's got all sorts of weapons lying in wait . . ."

Max narrowed his eyes. "Is that what's hidden under the sand?"

Spike wiggled his mouthparts in what Max guessed was a scorpion smirk. "Whatever's under there . . . I'm sure it'll make the lizards squirm."

As Max wondered what it could be, he and Spike and the termites approached the cliff's rocky foothills. As he swung off Spike, the great climb began. The termites had no trouble and swarmed up the rocky face in a living curtain of bugs. Even Spike scuttled merrily up, despite his weight.

Only Max found it hard going. He lagged behind the others, huffing and puffing, trying not to look down. He couldn't stop himself, though, and craned his neck to see the beach and the waves stretched out far below him. He wished he hadn't—the ground was very far away.

"Come on!" Spike urged from above.

I can do this, Max told himself. He clambered up the rocks, using strange little hollows in the cliff face as handholds. It looked like something had been burrowing in the crumbly cliff, creating dark little homes in the middle of the rock. But Max didn't stop to check; he was too busy trying to cling on for dear life.

Nearby, a clump of exposed grass roots dangled from a clump of earth. Max grabbed them and hauled himself up. But suddenly, the earth clump broke free and came loose from the rock face. Chunks of dirt fell and broke far beneath him.

"Spike, help!" he cried out.

But it was no use—Spike was too far

ahead to hear him. Max was left dangling from the side of the cliff, hanging on to a few flimsy grass roots. As he tried desperately to grab a fresh handhold, the first of the roots began to tear free . . .

BIG DIG

"Max!" bellowed Spike from above. He and the termites had made it to the top of the cliffs. "Are you all right?"

Max looked down again, feeling panicked. For the second time today he was high above the ground, but this time there was no water to fall into. These weren't called the Howling Cliffs for nothing—he'd be cut to ribbons on the fierce rocks below. He clung on to the roots with just one arm and tried not to focus on that.

"I'll be okay if I can just pull myself up . . ."

Max heaved himself up as hard as he could, trying to get to the handholds above, but as he did, more of the roots broke off in his hand.

"Don't just stand there, help him!" Spike roared to the termites, who had gathered to peer down at Max.

"Go!" the termites squeaked to one another. "Go, go, go!"

They swarmed over a nearby patch of vines and began to chomp away at it, biting a long length of vine free. It swung down like a rope, dangling above Max's head. It was almost—but not quite—close enough to grab.

The last root began to fray. It was now or never. Max kicked at the cliff face for a little more leverage and lunged at the vine with his free hand.

Got it!

He clung to the vine and swung out away from the rocks, then back against them, thudding against the hard surface. Max watched as the clump of broken roots tumbled down and crashed onto the sand far below.

"That was close," he muttered.

"Come on, Max!" Spike called. "You can do it!"

"He's only got four limbs," whispered a termite. "No wonder he can't climb very well."

Spike snapped one of his pincers threateningly. "He's doing just fine!"

Max was glad to hear Spike sticking up for him. His confidence surged. As if he'd been climbing a rope in gym class, Max hoisted himself up along the vine's length.

Spike helped him up the rest of the way, and eventually, Max pulled himself over the rim of the cliff. Brushing off the dirt and dust, he and Spike looked down at the terrifying drop below.

"Phew," Max said. "Hope I never have to do *that* again."

From the top of the Howling Cliffs, Max

could see the whole bay below. On the sand, the Battle Bugs were fortifying their defenses against attack from the sea. Ranks of praying mantises lined the beach like soldiers back in the real world. This cliff-top fortress was definitely going to be the perfect place to spy on any lizards preparing an attack—the bugs wouldn't be caught unprepared again.

Spike grabbed a rock in his pincer and dropped it down the cliff. "Good luck to any lizards trying to attack us from here," he said.

Max laughed. "I'd like to see them try. Let's get started on this watchtower."

Hundreds of termites were already streaming over the plateau at the top of the cliff, looking for the perfect place to build the tower. Right on the edge of the cliff, with a clear view of the bay, the ground leveled out into the perfect place for a dig.

"This'll do," grunted Razorjaw. "Plenty of nice, soft dirt to work with. All right, termites, get chewing!"

"Chewing?" Max asked.

All around, termites began stuffing their mouths with mud and dirt, and scurried into position.

"That's how we build," explained Razorjaw. "Worker termites fill their mouths up with dirt, then spit it back out again. Their saliva helps stick it all together." He trotted across to a patch of bare earth. "Want to try? Have a mouthful."

"No thanks," Max said, backing away.

"Hmph. Some bugs just love to watch someone else do all the work," a nearby worker grunted. He gulped up some dirt himself and went to build.

Max watched in fascination as the tower's foundations took shape. One termite on its own could place only a tiny blob of dirt, but thousands of them working together could build a massive structure. Soon, a brown wall higher than Max had taken shape on the cliff edge.

"We'll put an underground cavern in the middle and fill the whole thing with shelter tubes from bottom to top," Razorjaw told Max and Spike.

"Shelter tubes?" Spike asked, puzzled.

"That's our termite transport system! Or any other bugs, for that matter. Shelter tubes let you crawl around inside the mound and get to the top easily—that way we'll have no trouble spying on the enemy. Of course, I'm going to need some building materials, but I can't spare any workers to go get them."

"We'll go," Max offered.

"Great! There are two things I need: some plant material and some nice, fresh poop."

"Poop?" Max wished he hadn't offered!

"Yes!" said the termite irritably. "There's nothing better than dung for mixing with earth. Sets like a rock!"

"I'd rather just get you some plants," Max said with a shudder.

"Come on, shorty," said Spike. "Let's head into the jungle and get some leaves."

While a group of termites went off to collect dung, Max and Spike made their way farther back from the cliff edge. The huge Howling Cliffs soon made way for a thick expanse of jungle, and tall blades of grass and brightly colored flowers dwarfed Max once more.

"Grab some of those big green ones," Spike called, pointing to some dangling leaves. "They'll munch up nicely for the termites."

Max stood on Spike's back to pull down the branches, yanked off some leaves, and then impaled them onto Spike's tail. The scorpion grumbled a bit, but he had to admit it was a good way to carry as many leaves as they could.

As he stacked leaves on Spike's tail, Max had a sudden, creepy feeling of being watched. He whipped his head around, but couldn't see a thing—there was just the thick green jungle and the sound of bugs calling in the distance.

"Did you hear that?" Max asked.

"Nope," Spike mumbled cheerily. "Must be your imagination."

Max frowned—lizards had gotten every-where on Bug Island; that definitely wasn't his imagination. Maybe he shouldn't have used Spike as a leaf stacker—the scorpion couldn't use his tail to fight while he was carrying all those leaves with it.

But Max didn't actually see any lizards, so he and Spike continued deeper into the jungle. From time to time, he glanced up and thought he saw something darting out of sight, but it was so quick that it could have just been sunlight, shimmering through the canopy of leaves. Max shook his head and kept working until they reached a clearing. He gasped at the sight above him—something that even Spike couldn't miss.

Dangling high above, like giant raindrops suspended in the air, were dozens of chrysalises. Some were deep green in color; others were dusty brown with weird spikes running down their sides. Max had never seen anything like it.

"Spike! What are those?" Max asked, all thoughts of being watched in the jungle gone.

"Those are going to be butterflies!" he replied.

"Wow," Max said in awe. "How long until they emerge?"

"It shouldn't be too much longer. It looks like they're almost ready."

Max sighed, thinking back to when he'd unveiled his own costume at the birthday party. "I just hope I'm still on Bug Island when they come out. I wouldn't want to miss it!"

Later, at twilight, Max and Spike emerged from the jungle to an already impressive-looking tower. The chewed-up mud and earth had been transformed into a giant mound, perched on the edge of the Howling Cliffs. To Max, the whole thing looked like a sky-scraper under construction; hundreds of termites scurried around the structure at dizzying heights. Razorjaw barked orders to the construction team, and builder ter-mites put the finishing touches on the main structure.

Max gasped in admiration. "Wow!" he said. "That's some fortress!"

"No kidding!" Spike agreed as he stag-gered across to the foreman to offload the leaves.

"Not bad," Razorjaw barked, then turned to Max. "You'll want to inspect our work, no doubt. Should I show you around?"

"Definitely!" Max cried. "Spike, you stay here and help guard the workers."

Spike saluted.

The termite led Max inside a small hole in the mound and into a maze of tunnels. Max's head spun. He wondered how he'd ever remember which way was which. The main tunnel led into a large, cave-like meeting hall. The termites scurried in all directions, bringing in the leaves that he and Spike had collected to construct the tower's waterproof lining. Other tunnels snaked off the central chamber, spiraling up to where the watch station would be.

"This way leads to the observation deck," Razorjaw explained. "And down below is ammunition storage and emergency food supply."

"Wow," Max said. "It's so cool!"

But Max didn't have much time to stop and admire the termites' handiwork. A sudden yell came from the entrance tunnel.

"Alarm! Alarm!"

Max ran over to see what the problem was. The little termite he found was quivering in fear.

"G-g-geckos!" he stammered. "We're under attack!" The termite could barely get the words out, he was so terrified.

INTO THE MOUND

Max ran out of the mound and into the open area surrounding it. All of the termites were in chaos.

"Get inside the mound!" he yelled.

The termites crowded in through the tiny openings just as the first of the geckos scrambled over the cliff edge. Six or seven more quickly followed. The lizards were slender and long-tailed, with unblinking eyes that stared hungrily.

"How come the sentries didn't see them until just now?" Max shouted to the panicking termites.

A soldier termite shouted back to him: "They didn't climb up from the bottom. They were hiding inside the cliff the whole time!"

Hiding? Suddenly, Max thought back to the small handholds in the cliff wall that he'd used to haul himself up to the top—the geckos must have been waiting there to pounce! Even worse, Max looked toward the jungle where he and Spike had been foraging only moments before. He'd been certain they were being watched, and sure enough, a second wave of lizards came charging toward them from that direction, too. Multi-colored chameleons, with their long tongues flicking in all directions, lunged for the fleeing termites. It was a pincer attack: geckos on the left, chameleons on the right, and a deadly drop to the sea below them. There was no way to escape.

Spike charged the cliff edge, meeting the oncoming geckos head-on. "Bring it!" he roared. "I'll fight every one of you!"

"No, Spike! There's too many of them! Get inside!"

But the big scorpion wasn't listening. He grabbed two of the geckos, one in each pincer, and flung them backward over the edge of the cliff.

To Max's amazement, the lizards came scrabbling back up a moment later, with big smirks on their faces. Of course—geckos had unbelievably sticky feet and could cling to almost anything! No wonder they'd climbed the cliff so easily.

Spike jabbed his stinger into another gecko. The scorpion yelled in triumph, but even more geckos were arriving now. To make matters worse, the chameleon forces from the jungle had nearly reached the termite mound.

The last of the termites darted past Max and squeezed into the tunnel. "Come on, Spike!" he called desperately. "We can't fight this many!"

Spike finally seemed to realize he was

outnumbered. The geckos circled him, snapping their jaws, getting ready to rush him.

"Raaaargh!" bellowed Spike, charging forward.

His armored body smashed right through the startled geckos, like a runaway truck. One or two of them bit him, but not hard enough to get through his tough exoskeleton. Before they could regroup and attack, Spike had already broken their line and was hurtling full tilt toward the termite mound.

Max dived into the mound with Spike right behind him. He fell back against a heap of chewed leaves, just as Spike slammed into the opening. He squeezed himself halfway in, but then he got stuck.

"The termites didn't make the hole big enough for bugs like me!" he grunted. "Help me out!"

Together, Max and the soldier termites hauled Spike into the main underground chamber. A group of worker termites shot forward past him, their mouths packed with dirt. As Razorjaw and the other soldier termites nipped at the snarling geckos, the workers blocked up the hole.

Max breathed a sigh of relief. He looked around to see the termite workers cowering in the main chamber.

"What now?" Razorjaw asked him.

It dawned on Max that he was in charge. Barton had put him in command, and the survival of the watchtower was in his hands now.

"Fill up all the holes at ground level," he told Razorjaw. "Spike, you and I need to get a better look at the reptile forces—we can't let the watchtower fall into their hands. Or worse, let them destroy it. Let's head up to the observation deck."

Luckily, the upper tunnels were wide enough for Spike. The termites, knowing Max couldn't climb like a bug, had built a walkway in a spiral around the tower. It was easy, though exhausting, to run all the way up to the top deck.

Max found the observation deck the termites had made, complete with a landing platform and an impressive view across to the sea on one side and the jungle on the other. Looking down, he could see the geckos circling the mound, interspersed with hissing chameleons.

"I knew something was watching us in the jungle," Max muttered. "The chameleons must have been hiding in there, while the geckos were lurking in the cliff."

"Come out, come out!" called a rasping voice from down below. "The Howling Cliffs are *ours*."

Max looked down and saw one gecko, larger than the rest, grinning up at him.

"That's not gonna happen," Max said, folding his arms with determination.

The gecko leader laughed. "Have it your way! This miserable dunghill is now under siege. We're hungry—and we want *you* for dinner!"

Max stood thinking for a moment, and then turned to Spike. "Spike, call Razorjaw and the other soldier termites. We need to hold a council of war."

Down in the heart of the mound, the bugs gathered.

"What are we waiting for?" thundered Razorjaw. "The lizards attacked us, so we should attack them!"

"Fighting is all you soldiers understand," one of the workers said, wearily.

Razorjaw snapped his mandibles, making the worker jump.

"I know you're expert fighters, and brave, too," Max said carefully. "I wish we had a thousand more like you. But there just aren't enough of us."

"We're not scared of those lizards!" yelled a soldier termite. His fellow soldiers stomped and gnashed their jaws in agreement until Max signaled for silence.

Spike waved his pincer, and Max let him speak next.

"Let's make a break for it," the scorpion suggested. "Better to live to fight another day than get squashed."

"We could sprint down to the beach camp," agreed a soldier termite.

"Are you joking? Only a few of us would make it that far. We'd be eaten up!" argued the termite worker.

"Not if we fight our way out!"

"Most of us termites are builders, not fighters!"

Max struggled to think with the bugs arguing all around him. Obviously, they needed reinforcements. But Buzz wasn't due for her flyby until later, and Barton didn't even know the tower was under siege. Their best option was to try and escape.

"Wait!" he shouted. "I've got an idea."

The bugs fell silent. Countless sets of beady black eyes watched Max.

"If we can't fight our way out, maybe we can dig our way out," Max said. "We've got the best builders in all of Bug Island right here."

"That's a great idea," said Spike. Even the soldier termites nodded.

"Digging it is, then." The lead termite worker ran forward to lead the way, followed by his horde of fellow bugs. "After me!"

Together, Max and the bugs made their way down the termite structure, through the tunnels and ventilation shafts. Max looked admiringly at the termites' handiwork as they went. It was like being inside a bizarre alien planet from a science fiction movie.

As they drew closer to the base of the mound, a violent thump shook the walls.

"What was that?" Max wondered.

Before anyone could speak, another crash came, then another. Fragments of plant matter cracked and fell.

"It's the lizards! They're trying to get in," cried one of the workers. "We've got to hurry!"

Max ran ahead down the tubular passageway—and came face-to-face with a gecko!

"Going somewhere?" it hissed.

Max turned on his heels and ran back to the group. "Everyone get back!" he yelled. "Find a different way down."

"It's no good," came the muffled cry of a soldier termite. "The geckos are blocking all the downward tunnels!"

The dejected bugs had no alternative but to retreat. They made their way back to the central chamber and up toward the observation deck. Max sat in the middle while the termites went to work blocking off the lower tunnels, so the geckos couldn't climb any farther in.

"Now what?" Spike asked him.

Max had no answer to give. There was no way up, no way down, and the tower was slowly being demolished around them. The bugs were trapped.

UNDER SIEGE

A gloom settled over the group. The soldier termites hung their heads, and even Spike's mighty tail drooped in misery. The *crash*, *boom*, *crash* of geckos flinging themselves against the mound's walls never stopped.

"What are we going to do?" squeaked a little termite worker. "We can't go up, because we can't fly, and we can't go down, or the geckos will gobble us up."

"Maybe we should rush them after all," said Spike. "Go out in a blaze of glory."

"Not on my watch," said Max firmly. He stood up and dusted himself off.

"There's got to be something we're missing—some way out of here. Let's go back up top; maybe we can figure something out."

Max and the bugs made their way back to the upper deck of the mound and looked out from the observation deck. The sun had set and a bright moon now lit the land-scape. Many of the geckos and chameleons had lain down to rest, but a determined handful of them were still battering away at the mound.

"Comfortable up there, are you?" mocked the gecko leader.

"Come up here and see for yourself," Max shot back.

The gecko chuckled. "No need for that. Soon, you and all your friends will be brought down to earth with a bump. A very, very big bump."

Max feared he was right. The mound wasn't made to take this kind of punishment. It wasn't even fully finished. If the geckos kept up their pounding, it would collapse, crumbling into ruin, right over the edge of the Howling Cliffs and into the sea.

If that happened, it was game over.

Suddenly, a droning noise in the distance made him snap out of his gloom. He *knew* that sound. He craned his head back, look-ing up into the dark skies, praying he'd see a familiar sight zooming down toward him.

Sure enough, he soon caught sight of the yellow-and-black stripes he knew so well. "Spike, it's Buzz!" he shouted. "She's here!"

Spike cheered.

Max made his way up through the top-most shelter tubes all the way to the roof of the mound. The termites had done their best to create a wide, flat area surrounded by a low, bumpy wall. It was uneven and had holes in it, but it was good enough for Buzz to land on. Spike burst out behind Max on top of the watchtower.

Buzz hovered in the air and then descended like a helicopter on the deck, coming to rest with perfect precision. Max waved to her. "Am I glad to see you!"

"I saw the lizards as I flew over," Buzz reported. "Dozens of them. What on Bug Island is going on?"

"We're under siege," Spike cried. "Geckos came up the cliff and chameleons came from the jungle. They know how useful the watchtower would be to the Battle Bugs, and they want to destroy it before it's finished."

Max and Spike told Buzz all about the lizard attack, explaining how far inside the geckos had reached, while the hornet listened intently.

"We've got to break the siege," Buzz said once they'd finished. "Let me fly back to the beach camp. I can muster a battalion of bugs and bring them up here."

"No!" Max said quickly.

Buzz twitched one of her antennae. It looked just like a human raising an eyebrow in surprise. "No?"

"There are two reasons that's a bad idea: One, it'll take too long to bring them here, especially in the dark. Two, if you bring all the bugs up from the beach camp, you'll leave it undefended. For all we know, that's what Komodo wants us to do!"

"I see," Buzz said slowly. "This attack may be a trick, to get us to split our forces. We can't take the risk."

Max nodded. "It would put Barton himself in danger. That's not an option."

"Agreed," Spike said. "So what *do* we do?"

Max wracked his brains for an idea. Suddenly, looking down at his costume for Tyler's birthday party, he had a brain wave. *The man-faced stink bugs use their striking patterns to scare away predators—they don't have to fight them off; they don't even have to get close.* If there was some way of scattering the lizards and confusing their ranks, maybe the bugs inside the watchtower would have a chance to fight back or escape.

Then it struck him—the creatures he'd seen in the forest earlier. "I've got it," he called to Buzz. "I know the perfect bugs to help us out!"

*   *   *

The sun hadn't risen yet, but a muggy light in the east promised that it soon would.

Around the termite mound, a few sleepy, lethargic lizards kept up their siege, thumping at the now-battered walls. The rest lay still, waiting for the sun's warming rays to stir them to life.

Stealthily, Max, Buzz, and Spike clambered out onto the top of the termite mound. Max took a quick look over the edge to check on the lizards.

"What's wrong with them?" Buzz wondered. "Why are they so sleepy?"

"They're cold-blooded. Until the sun's energy gets them going, they're going to be slow and sluggish. That's why I wanted to leave at dawn."

"Good thinking!"

"Spike," Max said, turning to the scorpion. "You stay here and make sure the soldier termites are ready when we get back."

"Will do, Max," Spike called.

Max climbed onto Buzz's back and they took to the air. The geckos below them were so groggy they didn't even look up. Max grinned. *Perfect timing.*

"Where are we headed?" Buzz asked.

"Into the jungle," Max said. "I just hope there aren't any more of those chameleons waiting in the branches."

Buzz flew at breakneck speed, wind whistling through Max's hair, down the slope of the cliff and into the dark labyrinth of the jungle. This early in the day, Max could hardly see a thing, just the dim shapes of trees looming out of the shadows. Buzz confidently dipped and zoomed around them.

They were deep in the jungle when Max spotted what he was looking for. "Up there, Buzz! Those green chrysalises hanging from the branch—see them?"

"Locking on!"

Buzz pulled into a steep climb that almost flung Max off her bristly back and came in to land on the branch, right alongside the chrysalises. Max's heart sank. They were all empty. The butterflies he was counting on had already emerged and flown away.

"We're too late," he said. "That was my last idea."

Just then, sunlight began to seep in through the trees, brightening the jungle. As he felt the warmth on his skin, Max looked up and saw a distant, colorful flurry of wings down an avenue of trees.

"There they are. Go, go, go!"

Buzz whirled through the trees to where the butterflies fluttered in a crowded mass. Suddenly, Max was among some of the most stunning creatures he'd ever met. The colors of the butterflies' wings were like a pharaoh's treasure box: deep velvety reds, sapphire blues, greens and yellows like the sun on a summery field. But most striking of all were their eyespots, which were huge, circular markings that looked like the eyes of a much bigger predator. Being surrounded by the butterflies was like being stared at by eerie masks.

"Good to see you again, Admiral Peacock!" said Buzz. "You're not the caterpillar I used to know."

Admiral Peacock showed off her glorious wings. "I used to envy you, Buzz, with your ability to fly. Now, at last, I can fly myself."

"That's good, because we need your help. The new watchtower on the Howling Cliffs is under siege—if we can't repel the lizard forces, we're finished," Buzz continued.

"Butterfly squadron at your command," the admiral said, proudly.

"It's your eyespots, Admiral," Max chipped in. "I've seen other bugs with them

and they gave me an idea. They're for scaring away predators, right?"

"Yes. And they work fantastically well."

"So if the butterfly forces all swoop in and attack at the same time, we can scare away the geckos and reinforce the watchtower!"

Admiral Peacock hesitated. "It's worth a try. I warn you, though, we don't have stingers or pincers like the other fighters."

"You don't need them!" Buzz said. "We just need to panic them."

"Very well. Count us in!"

Max clapped his hands together. "Let's do this. Buzz, go get the rest of the hornet squadron. Admiral Peacock, arrange your troops into battle formation! Let's fly!"

Max climbed onto Admiral Peacock's back, and the colorful squad rose up as one, winging like shining kites through the morning air. The butterflies had barely hatched from their chrysalises, and already they were risking their lives for their fellow bugs.

Together, they flew through the jungle, making for the distant, dark shape of the termite mound.

BUG MONSTER

As the butterflies raced through the jungle and out onto the open plain of the Howling Cliffs, Max saw that the geckos and chameleons were wide awake. Now that the sun had risen fully and spurred them into life, the lizards were hard at work, ripping and biting at the walls of the mound.

Max heard the gecko leader yell at them to work harder. Huge craters had already appeared in the mound, and more muddy chunks broke free every moment. Soon, the whole construction would topple, falling over the cliff and smashing to bits far below.

"Faster!" Max yelled. "We have to stop them!"

Suddenly, as one, the butterflies dived toward the lizards like a living waterfall.

As the huge mass of fluttering wings descended upon them, one of the geckos raised the alarm in panic. "Look out!"

"What?" snarled the leader. He turned to look up and recoiled in terror.

Max urged Admiral Peacock to go faster.

He saw the glint of fear in the gecko's eyes and hoped that his lizard blood was running even colder.

The huge butterfly squadron looked like a shapeless, hovering mass with hundreds of eyes appearing and disappearing all at the same time. Maddening colors danced all through it. The gecko forces looked like they'd never seen anything like it, and never wanted to ever again.

"Get back!" the gecko shrieked to his forces. "It's some kind of bug monster! Retreat!"

Max, riding Admiral Peacock at the front of the "monster," laughed. The plan was working. Hundreds of butterflies swarmed around the geckos, fluttering their wings and showing their distinctive eyespots. To the lizards, it must have looked like a single terrifying creature. He couldn't blame them for running from a beast with a hundred staring eyes.

"Get closer," he urged the admiral.

Max could see Spike and the soldier termites peering out of the mound's upper spy holes. Max gave the sign to attack and Spike instantly obeyed, darting down into the termite mound, ready to lead the charge from the base of the structure.

The geckos and chameleons were scattered across the cliff top, thrown into complete disarray by the butterfly charge. But then, the young butterfly squadron began to separate and swoop down at the fleeing lizards without the protection of the group.

"No!" Admiral Peacock yelled. "We must stick together."

It was too late: A chameleon lashed out at an oncoming butterfly with his long tongue. The frail butterfly was smacked out of the air and fell, lying in a dizzy heap with its wings twitching.

"Sir!" bellowed the chameleon. "It's a trick!"

"What?" snarled the gecko leader, turning on his sticky heels.

"These bugs are as light as dandelion seeds. There's nothing to them."

Uh-oh, Max thought. *They're onto us . . .*

"Get back, you fools!" the gecko leader screeched. "Stop running. Attack them!"

"What now, Max?" Admiral Peacock asked, wheeling through the air.

The game was up, but at least the butterfly squadron had bought the bugs some time. Most of the lizards were still fleeing, and nearly all of them were in chaos. Using the butterflies' eyespots had evened up the numbers. Below, Spike was charging out of the mound, backed up by a mighty swarm of soldier termites. This might be a fight they could win after all!

"Admiral Peacock," Max cried, the wind whistling through his hair. "Can you bring me in close to Spike?"

"Consider it done."

The butterfly swept down to the head of the bug forces. Max leaped off her back and landed firmly on Spike's.

"Ready to rumble?" he asked the scorpion.

"I thought you'd never ask," Spike said happily.

"CHARGE!"

Spike went galloping into battle on his eight powerful legs. He snatched at the confused geckos, crushing with his pincers and jabbing with his stinger.

All around, bugs and lizards clashed in fierce combat. Soldier termites swarmed over geckos, nipping with their strong jaws. Nimble butterflies darted in and out, distracting the lizards while other bugs struck at them. Max yelled orders from Spike's back, sending the bug troops to strike at retreating targets.

We just need to break their determination, he thought. *But how?* The bugs were *almost* winning, but not quite. He needed something to tip the balance.

A buzzing, droning noise from above answered his question. "It's Buzz!" he yelled. "And the hornet squadron!"

The geckos and chameleons were having a bad morning already. First, the butterflies had terrified them. Then the bugs, who were supposed to be terrified and hiding in their watchtower, had fought back. Now a whole squadron of angry hornets was power-diving at them. Their bad morning had just become a lot worse.

It was too much for the gecko leader. "Geckos and chameleons retreat," he yelled. "If Komodo wants this watchtower so badly, he can come and take it himself."

The humiliated lizards scrambled down the edge of the cliff or back into the jungle where they'd come from. Max patted Spike on his back, and the termite soldiers cheered. Some of the hornets got quick stings in for good measure.

"And stay out!" Buzz shouted to the last fleeing chameleon.

"You've done it, Max!" Razorjaw hopped up and down with joy. "The watchtower's saved!"

BEACH BATTLE

Crowds of termite workers squeaked and ran around excitedly, cheering their victory. However, there wasn't much time for celebrations—the bugs had a position to fortify. A platoon of soldier ants, the closest forces Buzz had been able to reach, came trooping up the slope to reinforce the tower. Termite workers made repairs.

It wasn't long before Max was standing at the top of the tower, looking out across the sea toward the lava bridge and the distant mass of Reptile Island. Buzz and Spike stood by his side.

"Next time the lizards attack, we'll see them coming," Buzz said.

A movement on the water caught Max's eye. He looked closer.

"That might be sooner than we think!" Max cried. "Do you see what I see?"

Spike gasped. "Basilisk lizards!" A whole group of the lizards was racing across the water. This was no scouting party. This was a full-on invasion force.

Max realized this was the second half of a one-two punch from Komodo. First, the geckos were meant to tear the tower down, and then the basilisk lizards would swarm the island.

"We need to warn Barton, fast," Max called, leaping onto Buzz's back. He shouted back to the scorpion, "Spike, I'll go with Buzz—we'll meet you on the beach!"

"Sure thing, human bean," Spike called.

Buzz powered up her wings and zoomed down the side of the cliff, with Max hanging on for dear life. She pulled out of her crash dive and shot out across the bay like a missile. She would never usually fly so fast, but they had to reach Barton before the lizard forces landed on the beach—or Bug Island was finished.

The pair of them flew down across the bay, just slightly above the water's surface. Waves rose and fell and frothy foam spewed out into the air—Max grabbed on to Buzz as securely as he could.

"Look!" Buzz yelled above the sound of her wings. "Our fishing spider forces are out on patrol!"

Max was glad to see the spiders skittering back and forth across the water, ready for anything that might come toward the land. They were like explosive mines bobbing about in the deep sea, waiting for enemy ships to smash into them unawares.

Barton's temporary camp came into view, and Buzz rocketed toward it. She and

Max slammed into a mossy landing pad, sending both of them tumbling over and over before coming to an abrupt stop.

Max opened his eyes to see Barton and his praying mantis guard looking down at him with concern. "Are you all right? That was quite a smash."

"General, you need to prepare the troops. A lizard invasion force is coming!"

Max quickly explained what he'd seen from the watchtower.

Barton grimaced. "In that case, we must defend the beach at all costs! The watch-tower plan has worked better than we could have foreseen," he told Max as they walked together. "I cannot believe it was almost destroyed. The reptile spies must have heard us planning."

"There were chameleons in the jungle," Max said. "They make the best spies."

Down at the beach, the bugs lined up in their battle ranks. The toughest, most armored bugs went in the front row. That line was mostly beetles and scorpions, who could withstand the lizards' ferocious assault. On the sides, the hard-hitting striker bugs lurked, waiting to attack and withdraw: the mantises, bombardier beetles, and Webster's spider troop. Finally, the hornet squadrons waited at the very rear, ready for the order to fly.

From out at sea, one of the fishing spiders

skipped back toward the shore: "Lizards sighted!"

"Give me types and numbers!" Barton bellowed.

"There's a troop of geckos crossing the lava bridge—chameleons, too. Komodo is right in the middle of them, and the basilisk lizards are following."

They're coming at us from all sides! Max thought.

The fishing spiders fell back to the beach to join the rest of the bug forces as General Komodo drew closer.

Komodo and his gecko platoon, followed by the chameleons and basilisk lizards, slithered off the lava bridge and into the shallows. They splashed up onto the sandy beach, glaring at the assembled bugs.

"I see you were expecting us," Komodo said. "So nice of you to prepare dinner!"

"We saw you coming, all right," Max called.

"Of course. That pointless watchtower you built on the cliff. What a waste of time! You should know by now that we lizards are everywhere. You'll need more than that to keep us off *our* island."

"This is *Bug* Island," Max cried. "And we plan to keep it that way!"

"We'll see about that," Komodo hissed.

Barton grunted and opened his hardened wing cases. "I've heard enough," he cried. "Battle Bugs, attack!"

The front rank of beetles charged down the beach and plowed into the gecko ranks. Their pincers nipped and bit, making the geckos hiss in anger. In retaliation, the lizards swatted at the beetles, trying to tip them over onto their backs, where they would be helpless. Komodo lunged down with his massive jaws, snapping up beetles and flinging them aside.

Spike came scuttling across the sand toward Max. "I came as fast as I could!"

"You haven't missed the fight," Max assured him. Together, they rode down to the front lines.

"Mantises!" Max yelled. "This way!"

The mantises raced over. Max directed them toward the chameleons, leading the attack himself from Spike's back. In a flurry of snapping pincers, lashing venomous barbs, and vicious claw attacks, the chameleons were forced back to the water's edge. Their color-changing abilities did nothing to stop them from being beaten in this fight.

Out on the water, the fishing spiders were doing their best to keep the basilisk lizards at bay, but they were hopelessly out-sized. The lizards came splashing toward the shore, their eyes filled with an evil hunger.

Max remembered when he'd swum to the shore, chased the whole way by the basilisk lizard. Barton had told him about a reserve force buried in the sand. Now would be the perfect time to use it. "Barton!" Max yelled.

"That secret weapon you mentioned? Now might be the time to use it."

"I think you're right, Max," Barton called out. He made a piercing, high-pitched noise. Max covered his ears.

Up from the sand a volley of winged, hunched-over bugs burst into the air. They had long mouthparts, skinny bodies, and bristly legs.

Max gasped. "Assassin flies!" He knew they could deliver a nasty bite and their huge proboscis was full of toxins that could paralyze their prey—they were vicious predators.

"Dive!" buzzed their leader. The cloud of assassin flies rushed into the fight, swarming around the lizards' faces and blinding them. They bit where they could, one of them even landing a hit on Komodo himself.

"*Rargh!* Where are those basilisks?" Komodo roared. "Finish these wretched bugs now!"

Max looked around to see the basilisk lizards wading through the sea-foam up toward the shore. The fishing spiders were limping back inland, desperately trying to keep them from landing.

The geckos saw their reinforcements coming and cheered. Max's heart sank. The bugs had been so close to victory . . . If they couldn't beat the lizards back, Bug Island would surely become a second Reptile Island!

BRIGHT IDEA

"We need your brains, Max," said Spike as he wrestled an attacking gecko with his pincers. "Do you have any bright ideas?"

From Spike's back, Max could clearly see the gecko struggling, biting, and clawing for all it was worth. The lizard's long tail dangled below, trailing in the sand.

Compared to Spike's proud, stinger-bearing tail, it was useless.

Wait, Max thought, suddenly remembering something about geckos. If they were attacked on the tail, they could detach it from their body to escape. But not having a tail left them off-balance and unable to fight as fiercely as usual.

"Spike, grab his tail!" Max yelled.

Spike seized the gecko's tail in his pincer. Instantly, it fell off, like a limp rope. The gecko seemed to go crazy with fear.

"Argh!" it yelled. "My tail! Help!" With that, it sprinted back down the beach, toward the bridge.

Max grinned. His trick had worked. The geckos' survival instincts wouldn't let them stay in a fight if they had lost their tails. The urge to flee was just too strong.

"Bugs, aim for the geckos' tails and hang on!" he called out.

The bugs passed the message along the beach, then went to work. Mantises grabbed gecko tails and pinned them tight until they fell off. Scorpions followed Spike's example, grabbing a gecko tail in each strong pincer. As the geckos' tails came loose, the lizards went into a blind panic, fleeing away as fast as they could. Some of them even crashed back into the sea, floundering in the waves.

Komodo let out an angry roar. The beach in front of him was littered with dropped tails. The lizards he'd counted on to lead his

attack were running in terror. The bugs advanced, marching steadily as Komodo fell back step-by-step toward the lava bridge.

The chameleons were down, and the geckos were running away. Only Komodo's loyal basilisk lizards remained, and they were looking less loyal by the second, glancing fearfully at one another. When the assassin flies and hornet squadrons swept in to attack from two sides at once, it was too much. The basilisks turned and ran.

"ARGHH!" Komodo roared, backing away across the lava bridge once more. "This isn't over, Barton. One day, I swear, I will devour you. Bite by bite!"

"Speaking of bites," Barton said, "you're about to get a few more of your own. Assassin flies, escort General Komodo off *our* island!"

The swarm of assassin flies surrounded Komodo, biting him everywhere they could and making him howl. Max watched him vanish over the horizon, with the flies chasing him all the way.

A cheer went up from the bugs on the beach. "Victory!"

"You've done it again, my young friend," Barton said. "Bug Island will never fall to the lizards. Not while we have you on our side."

*   *   *

Now that the bugs were safe, Max was eager to return to Tyler's birthday party. After a swift good-bye, he held his magnifying glass up to the sky. He felt himself rushing up into the air as strange forces pulled him away from Bug Island and back to his own world.

As he whirled giddily through the air, he suddenly wondered what would happen if he came out high above the ground in the real world, like he had in Bug Island. He'd be smashed to a pulp! Surely the *Encyclopedia* knew what it was doing . . . right?

With a pop, he fell back into reality. To his horror, he was still falling. He *had* come out in midair.

In the next second, there was a mighty *twang* as Max hit Tyler's backyard trampoline. He shot back up into the air, landed again, bounced up and down, and eventually came to a wobbly stop. The birthday party was still in full swing.

Tyler was staring at him with his mouth wide open.

"How did you do that? You went into my house, then the next thing I know, you're out here!" He frowned. "You didn't jump out of the window, did you?"

"Nope," said Max with a wink. "You must have just missed me. I'm sneaky like that."

Tyler looked puzzled, and shook his head. "Come on. I need you in my Fortress of Power. We're playing capture the flag and

I need a second-in-command. You up for the job?"

"Count me in!" Max said, laughing. *After all*, he thought, *I've got plenty of siege experience now!*

REAL LIFE BATTLE BUGS!

Emperor Scorpion

The emperor scorpion is one of the largest scorpions in the world. It has long been feared by humans for its unusual size and strong claws—however, it's one of the less venomous species of scorpion in existence.

Although not fatal to humans, the scorpion's sting is effective against its prey, which is primarily termites. The emperor scorpion has been known to dig down as far as six feet in order to reach its favorite morsel.

Fishing Spider

This kind of spider is most at home in or around water. Found across North America, Europe, and New Zealand, fishing spiders use their incredible abilities to hunt aquatic insects, and even small fish, to survive.

The fishing spider is hydrophobic. This doesn't mean that it is *scared* of water; instead, it means that it *repels* water. The spiders are covered in tiny hairs that allow them to dash across the water without them actually making contact with it. If a fishing spider needs to dive, these hairs provide a thin coating of trapped air around its body, keeping the spider beneath nice and dry!

Admiral Butterflies

The red admiral is a relatively common butterfly found across large swaths of Europe, North America, and Asia. Its striking black wings with red stripes and white eyespots make it one of the most recognizable and well-known butterfly species.

Before it turns into a butterfly, the red admiral caterpillar is not to be messed with. Their black-and-yellow bodies are protected by rows and rows of branched spikes. Any bird or other predator that tries to eat them will get a pointy surprise!

THE ADVENTURE CONTINUES!

Max Darwin is summoned back to Bug Island to discover the island in turmoil. Spike has vanished, and his disappearance has all the hallmarks of one of General Komodo's schemes.

Max soon discovers that Spike has been bugnapped and is being held prisoner by the enemy. The Battle Bugs have no choice but to head straight into the heart of the Reptilian Empire!